Love Me Home

Tawdra Kandle

Published by Tawdra Kandle, 2018.

This is a work of fiction. Similarities to real people, places, or events are entirely coincidental.

LOVE ME HOME

First edition. May 18, 2018.

Copyright © 2018 Tawdra Kandle.

ISBN: 1719360332

Written by Tawdra Kandle.

To all of the readers who fell in love

with Burton, Georgia

Love Me Home

Before Meghan met Sam . . . before Jude loved Logan . . . there was another crossover romance between Crystal Cove and Burton.

When Sasha Jones was eight years old, her grandmother rescued her from a dangerous home and whisked her off to Crystal Cove, where Sasha grew up and fell in love with local boy Cole Wilson.

Fourteen years after she left her Georgia hometown, Sasha makes the painful choice to go back to take care of the mother who'd abandoned her. But making this decision means losing Cole when he can't understand why she needs to do it.

Cole knows Sasha is worth his patience. But when she makes a move that threatens their future together, he realizes he can't wait any longer. He's tired of playing games. He'll do anything to remind her where she belongs.

Is his love enough to bring her home?

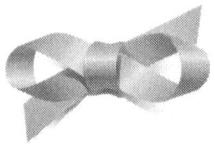

Prologue

SASHA

"You don't get to decide this time, Cole. You don't control me. You're not the one in charge."

I stomped my foot, mostly because I was so angry that it just had to come out some way. It might have been childish, but it was better than throwing something . . . which wasn't outside of the realm of possibilities, either. If we'd been fighting at my house, I might've done just that. But since we were in Cole's apartment above the RipTide, I still had enough presence of mind to behave.

"Sasha, what the hell is going on in your head? I can't believe you're seriously considering this." Cole raked his fingers through his hair, a gesture I usually found adorable. Right now, it was annoying the shit out of me.

"I'm not just considering it. I'm doing it. I'm moving up to Burton . . . for as long as I need to be there. And there's nothing you can say or do to stop me." I sniffed, but I wasn't going to cry. "Honestly, I thought you'd understand why I have to do this."

"Oh, did you? I guess you overestimated my capacity for making sense of idiocy. Sorry." Sarcasm tinged his voice.

"Cole, you love your mom, don't you? Wouldn't you do anything for her?"

He stared me down. "Of course, I would, and you know it. But that's not the same thing. My mother never abandoned me.

She didn't leave me with a man who hit me, who exposed me to drugs and tried to sell me for his next score."

I flinched. "She was sick. She didn't know what she was doing. She wasn't much more than a kid herself when she had me."

"Uh huh. Tell me, Sash. If we had a baby right now, would you leave her in danger, just because it was convenient for you?"

That stung. I sucked in a breath. "You know I wouldn't. But I'm not sixteen. I'm twenty-two. And I was raised by—" I stopped abruptly. That argument wouldn't fly, because the truth was that I'd been raised by the same woman who'd brought up my mother. The fact that I'd turned out better than Lorene could be chalked up to any number of causes—gratitude that Gram had saved me from a deplorable situation, lessons Gram had learned from my mom's childhood that she'd applied to mine or maybe simply a difference in temperaments. Regardless, I wasn't going to debate the point with Cole right now.

"Sasha." Cole reached for me, his hands gripping my upper arms. "Babe, I'm not trying to make you feel bad. I'm just saying that what you're talking about is crazy. You get a call from Georgia, from someone who tells you that your mother, who you haven't seen since you were, what? Six?"

I pressed my lips together. "Four," I murmured.

"Four," Cole echoed. "So almost twenty years have gone by since she took off without you. And now she's sick, she went back to her hometown, and she doesn't have anyone else, so you're supposed to drop your own life and run up there to be her nursemaid? And that sounds like it makes sense to you?"

"It doesn't make sense. You're right. But sometimes love isn't sensible." I lifted my eyes to stare into his. "When you met me, we were eight. You hated me—"

"I didn't hate you. I never hated you."

I went on as though he hadn't spoken. "I remember that day like it was yesterday. Your dad was taking you fishing on the intercoastal, and you were so excited... until he told you that I was coming, too. Then you said you didn't want to go if some stupid girl had to be there. You told him you hated me."

The ghost of a smile crossed his lips. "I probably did. I was a little moron. And I thought all girls were disgusting. But after that day on the boat, we were friends."

"Yes," I agreed. "We were. We were friends for a long time, until we weren't."

"Until we were more than friends. Until we fell in love." He nudged my chin up. "And that was the best thing that ever happened to me."

I swallowed over the lump in my throat. "It was for me, too. But no one else understood, did they? Your friends—back in elementary school, some of them thought you were crazy for hanging around with the weirdo girl from Georgia. It was the same way in high school. Cole, you could've had any girl in Crystal Cove. You still could. That you chose me didn't make any sense."

He frowned. "That's not the same situation."

"Maybe it doesn't seem that way to you, but it does to me. You loving me . . . that's just the craziest thing I ever knew. It's probably as unbelievable as me feeling like I have to go to Burton to take care of Lorene."

"I don't get it." Cole shook his head. "What about us, Sasha? What am I supposed to do? Sit down here and twiddle my thumbs while you're living in Georgia? I thought we were making plans. I thought—" He broke off, and I saw pain flicker in his eyes.

"We are." I wrapped my arms around my middle and stood silently for a moment. "Come with me, Cole. You'd love Burton. When I went up there last weekend, I really liked the town. It's like the Cove, only without the ocean. The people are friendly, and we could make all our plans there. It's just a change of venue."

"I don't want to move." He dropped his hands from me and turned around, hunching his shoulders. "I love the Cove. This is my home." He glanced back at me. "I thought it was your home, too."

"It is." I twisted the small silver ring on my right hand, the one Cole had given me when we graduated from high school. It was a claddagh, and he'd told me that night that this ring represented a promise. It meant that he was never going to leave me—that we'd be together for always. We'd both been sure that we were too young for diamonds and weddings back then, but Cole had an uncanny knack for realizing what I was thinking and feeling even before I did. He'd known that I needed a tangible sign of assurance that he was committed to me.

"Crystal Cove is the home that welcomed me when I was young and scared and lonely. The people here never made me feel like a freak, even when I was sure I was one. Of course, I love this place." I struggled to put into words what I wanted to say. "It's always going to be my safe landing spot. It's where Gram is. And it's where you are. If I hadn't gotten this call . . . I probably wouldn't have ever thought about leaving. But I did, and now I have to go back."

"You don't *have* to. You're choosing to go." There was clear accusation in his tone.

"You're right. I am choosing to go. But if I don't do this, Cole—if I turn my back on this chance to help my mother and to get to know her, I won't be the person you love. If I were the type of woman who could ignore her own flesh and blood, no matter what she did to me, you wouldn't love me, because I wouldn't be me."

He scowled. "That's bullshit. Putting yourself in a place where she can hurt you again is—it's masochism. I'm not going to stand by and watch you suffer, Sasha. You can't ask me to do that. It's not fair."

I took a deep breath. "You're right, it isn't. But I'm going up there, Cole. If you can't be supportive, then I understand."

"What's that supposed to mean?" His eyebrows drew together, and those warm brown eyes went dark and stormy.

"Maybe we need to take a break. Like you said, I can't expect you to sit around here and wait for me, and I can't promise when I'll be back. I'm staying in Burton as long as Lorene needs me. So I'm releasing you from your promise." Tears choked me, even as I struggled to twist the ring off my finger.

"Don't you dare give that back to me. Don't you dare." Cole spoke low. "That was a gift, Sasha. And everything it stood for—I still mean it."

I closed my fingers into a fist. "All right. I'll keep it, but Cole, I won't hold you to anything. Life has to go on. If things work out and I come back and you still want me, then that's wonderful. But if you don't, I understand." I took a step toward him and laid my hand on his wrist. "I'm leaving first thing in the morning, so this is goodbye."

"I'm not kissing you goodbye." He shook me off. "I won't do it. Think about this, Sasha. Promise me you will. Take a few days."

"I don't need to think about it. I know what I'm doing." I waited a few minutes, but he didn't answer. "I need to go now."

He stared at the wall, obstinate as always. I surrendered and headed for the door, pausing just long enough on the threshold for one last look.

"Good-bye, Cole."

Chapter One

COLE

Six Months Later

"Hey, Cole! Is this your phone?" Jude lifted the cell in one hand. "It's been ringing non-stop in the back."

"Yeah, it's mine." I reached for an empty glass in the corner of the bar. "Sorry about that. I must've forgotten to turn it off when I came in."

"It's not a problem, hon. Maybe you should check it, though, just in case something's wrong. Someone's clearly trying to get through to you." My boss patted my shoulder and set down the phone in front of me. "We're pretty quiet right now, anyway."

"I'm sure it can wait—" As if on cue, the phone began to buzz and ring again, vibrating against the scarred wood of the bar. I glanced down at the readout on the screen and frowned. "Uh, actually, Jude, can I take my break now?"

"Of course. You can go out on the deck—it's empty at the moment."

I nodded my thanks, answering the call as I walked quickly around the bar and headed through the screen door that led to the outdoor seating section.

"Gram, what's up?"

"Cole. Thank heavens. I've been trying to get through to you all afternoon." She sounded breathless, and my heart dropped through my stomach.

LOVE ME HOME

"What's wrong? Is it Sasha?" I gripped the phone until my fingers hurt.

"As a matter of fact, it is." She sighed heavily. "I'm sorry to bother you, Cole, but I couldn't sit around and not say anything. It just wouldn't be right."

"Is she sick? Is she hurt?" I jammed my fingers through my hair and squinted against the waning rays of the sun.

"No, no, nothing like that. I'm sorry, I didn't mean to alarm you. She's all right, physically at least. But she's about to make a huge mistake." Gram paused. "I think she's going to marry him."

The world spun around me, and I leaned against the railing that surrounded the deck. "Who is she going to marry?"

"His name is Sam Reynolds. He's a farmer."

"Sasha is marrying a farmer? Since when? And why? How the hell did this happen?" I kicked at the leg of a chair, frustrated. "She wasn't supposed to meet someone up there. She was just supposed to go up there, take care of that woman and then come back home—to me."

"I know, honey, I know." Gram's voice was soothing, even though I could still hear the worry behind it. "That's exactly why I came up to Georgia last month. She's been away too long. Someone had to shake sense into her. And since you refused . . ."

"I told you I wouldn't go chasing after Sasha. She made it very clear when she left that she didn't need me, and I'll be damned if I go crawling up there like I'm her lapdog." *Yeah, I was still just a little bitter.*

"Yes. I get it, but at the same time, if we let her sit up here brooding, she'll never go back to the Cove. And you and I both know what Sasha's like. She's dang stubborn. Even if she realized that she'd been wrong about going to Burton, she'll never admit it."

I ran my hand over my face. "What am I supposed to do, Gram? I'm not sure why you're calling me now."

She made a noise of impatience. "We're not going to let her make a mistake like this. My granddaughter has loved you forever. If I've ever known two people meant to be with each other . . . you two would be it. This is just a bump in the road. If you don't go after her, Cole, you're both going to regret it."

I knew she was right. It didn't make the decision any easier. "Can't you talk sense into her? You're her grandmother. She's supposed to listen to you, because you're wise and all that."

"Cole, you've known this girl just about as long as I have. You were the first person she met when I took her away from that hellhole her father had her in and brought her down to the Cove. When has she ever listened to me?"

I exhaled long. "Yeah, I guess you're right. But what am I going to do? Just show up?"

"Yes." Gram was firm. "You get your fine booty up here and remind her about what she's missing at home. You can stay at Millie and Boomer's house with me. I already checked with Millie, and she said it's fine. Her two oldest girls are off at college now, so she has the space."

"I could always get a motel room. Let's face it—if Sasha doesn't want to see me or tells me that we're really over for good, I'm not going to want to hang out up there." I tried to ignore the pang of hurt at the thought of my girl turning me away once and for all.

"You can't look at this as an ultimatum, Cole. Listen to me, now. The more you demand, the more she's going to get her back up. You're going to have to romance her. Woo her. Remind her why she fell in love with you in the first place." Gram cleared her throat. "It's a marathon, not a sprint."

"Great. So, I'm supposed to put my life on hold to convince my girlfriend that she should still love me?" I stared out at the ocean, waving in its endless loop of ebb and flow. "I have a job, Gram. I have *two* jobs. Remember? Those are the things that pay the bills. I need to hold onto these jobs if I want to start my own business. We've got goals—or at least, we did before Sasha took off. Maybe now those are only mine."

"She still wants those plans and dreams, sweetheart. She only has to remember that she does. As for your jobs, I think you can afford to take off a week. You've got to have some vacation time coming to you. Jude and Daniel are both fair-minded people, and if you explain, I know they'll understand."

Gram wasn't wrong. My job with Daniel Hawthorne was full time, which meant I was entitled to a week of vacation every year—and in the four years I'd been with his company, I'd never taken time off.

"I'll talk to them and see, and then I'll let you know what I'm going to do." I paused. "Don't let her do anything stupid before I get to Georgia, okay?"

"I'll do what I can. But don't dawdle, Cole. Don't waste any time getting here."

"I'll be in touch," I repeated. "Thanks for calling, Gram."

"Be careful, honey. I'll see you soon." She disconnected the call, and I stood still for a moment, gazing down the beach, before I turned around and stalked back into the restaurant.

Jude's daughter, Meggie, sat at the bar, her math book open and a pencil in her hand flying across a notebook page. She glanced up as I came in, and her face flushed pink. She'd just turned thirteen, and in the past few months, she'd developed an adorable crush on me. At least, I saw it as adorable. She was a cute little girl, and someday, I knew she'd make some man very happy. In the meantime, I did whatever I could to be kind without encouraging her at all.

"Is it Sasha?" she asked now, her eyes sympathetic. She had the same expression on her face that most people around the Cove did these days when they saw me. *Poor Cole, who'd been thrown over by his girlfriend, who'd left him to run away to Georgia.*

"Uh, yeah. I mean, no, it wasn't her on the phone—it was her grandmother."

Meggie grinned. "Oh, I love Miss Dixie. Is everything okay?"

I frowned, preoccupied. "Yeah. She's just . . ." I shook my head and looked around for Jude. "Dixie's fine, and so is Sasha. Where's your mom?"

"Kitchen." She tilted her head. "Are *you* okay, Cole?"

"Sure. Just dandy." I winked at Meggie to show my pissiness wasn't aimed at her and went into the kitchen behind the bar.

Jude was scraping the grill, grimacing at the effort, but she smiled as I came in. "Everything all right, Cole?"

"Sure," I began and then stopped, shaking my head. "Actually, no. Jude, I hate to do this, but I might need to take a week and go up to Georgia. That was Miss Dixie on the phone. Sasha . . . she's . . . well, there's this guy. And he's a farmer, and Gram—that is, Miss Dixie says Sasha's going to marry him." Even saying the words out loud to someone else was painful.

"Well, that's ridiculous," Jude answered me crisply. "Sasha loves *you*, Cole. She's never had eyes for another man. Maybe Dixie's jumping to conclusions."

"Sasha might love me, but she's also hard-headed. I wouldn't put it past her to stay up there and marry some man just to spite me." God knew I loved Sasha beyond reason, but I wasn't blind to her faults. Hell, we'd known each other so long that I was also aware of the genesis of those faults. The first eight years of her life had been a horror show, and no one escaped that kind of situation unscathed.

"Then I guess you better get your ass up there and make sure that doesn't happen." Jude set down the scraper and wiped her hands on her apron. "I hope you know me well enough to realize that you don't have to worry about your job while you're gone. It'll be here waiting for you."

"Thanks, Jude." I cracked my neck, trying to ease some of the tension there. "Now I just need to talk to your husband about taking the time."

"If I say you can go, you better believe Daniel will agree. I know that your work with him is your main job, but he's not going to tell you no. Besides, don't you have some vacation days built up?"

I smirked. "A couple, I guess. Or maybe, like . . . four weeks. I was saving them. I had this crazy idea that when Sasha and I finally tied the knot, I could take her on a real kick-ass honeymoon, and I'd need the time for that."

"And you will. But take a week now. If you need more, take more. When you're ready for the kick-ass honeymoon, Daniel and I will make sure you have it. Trust me, Cole. You're one of the good guys. You're conscientious, smart and loyal. We're not going to risk losing you."

I cocked my eyebrow. "Even when I finally get enough money to open my own place and become your competition?" It was a running joke between Jude and me. I'd never made any secret of the fact that I wanted to run my own restaurant eventually, though what I had in mind was nothing like the Tide.

"Bring it, son." She narrowed her eyes, but she couldn't hold the fake scowl for long before she started giggling. "Cole, when you finally open your barbecue joint, Daniel and I will be there, cheering you on. You know that's how we roll in the Cove. Plus, I'll just be excited to have a place to eat on my days off."

"Funny, I don't think I've ever seen you take a day off, Jude."

She nodded and held a finger to her lips. "Shhhh. I'm going to tell you a secret. Days off are for people with jobs. The RipTide isn't my job. It's my way of life. After Daniel and Meggie and Joseph—and the posse—the Tide is my family. I can't imagine living without it."

"Glad to see we made it in ahead of your restaurant, Jude." A low, dry voice startled both Jude and me, and we turned around in unison. Logan Holt was lounging in the doorway between the bar and the kitchen.

I'd known Logan for as long as I had Jude and Daniel. Like my bosses, he was a major player in the community of Crystal Cove. He was an architect with his own firm, and he often worked with Daniel's contracting company. I'd seen the two men hanging out together on job sites.

Not only that, along with four other local men who'd all been friends since grade school, they formed what they called the posse. It was a term they used mostly in jest, though I knew the relationships were deep and abiding.

"Jesus, Logan. You scared me to death." Jude rolled her eyes. "That's it. You've now dropped in status . . . somewhere below the Tide and above . . . hmmmm." Her smile was wicked. "Karlee."

Logan's face fell, and he backed away slowly. "You're saying that when it comes to important people in your life, I'm just a little above Cooper's nut job ex-wife? Thanks, Jude. Way to wound one of your best friends."

"You asked for it, sneaking up on Cole and me like that." She folded her arms over her chest. "Did you need something, or did you just come back to harass me?"

"Just came by to say hello. I stopped for a beer before my meeting with your lesser half."

"Ah, that's right." Jude nodded. "You and Daniel are going to figure out what properties you're buying next, huh?"

"That's the plan." Logan tugged at the knot in his tie, loosening it a bit. "I'm pitching a new office complex over the bridge, and Daniel's still talking about that house down the street here."

"Ohhhh." Jude's face lit up. "I love that old place. I think the two of you restoring it would be amazing. I told Daniel it would be a perfect bed and breakfast. The town needs something like that."

Logan studied Jude, and I saw conflict in his gaze. "It's not that I don't agree, but right now, getting the property is a problem. The estate of the last owner has dug in its heels, and they're asking more than it's worth. I think with a little patience, we'll be able to wait them out and get it for a decent price. It's not that I don't agree with you and Daniel. I just think we need to bide our time."

"I trust you." Jude smiled and glanced at me. "Sorry, Cole. Didn't mean to derail our talk—blame Logan."

"It's not a problem. If you're sure it's okay for me to miss my shifts for a week, I think I'll go talk to Daniel before his meeting. If he gives me a green light, I'll pack tonight and head to Georgia first thing in the morning."

"He's going to tell you the same thing I just did, but I know you, Cole. You need to hear it for yourself." She waved her hand. "Go on. Be careful driving up there and let me know when you arrive. You know I'll worry."

"Mother hen Jude," Logan teased. "Always worried about all the chicks."

I laughed. "I promise, Jude. I'll call tomorrow and keep you posted on what happens."

"You do that." She paused, and her eyes met mine with steady certainty. "Bring home your girl, Cole. It's time she was back in the Cove."

Chapter Two

SASHA

The breeze that brushed over my face as I sat on the Reynolds' front porch was just cool enough to be refreshing. It carried with it a certain unique aroma that brought to mind a memory I couldn't quite access. It was definitely the smell of a farm, I decided; although Sam and Ali Reynolds didn't keep animals on their property, their neighbors, the Nelsons, had horses. But it was more than that. It was a mix of freshly turned soil, of ripening fruit and of waving grass warmed by the sun.

I wondered if I'd spent any time on a farm when I was little, before my mom had left. For a moment, I considered asking Lorene about that, but the odds were good that she wouldn't remember—and if she said she did, chances were also good that she wouldn't be telling me the truth.

Swallowing a sigh, I closed my eyes and leaned back on the swing, rocking it gently with the toe of one foot pressed against the worn wood of the floor. These six months in Burton had been . . . a challenge. My mother's decades of alcoholism and addiction had left her physically frail and mentally unstable. She'd been diagnosed with an illness that would eventually take her life, but until then, she needed almost constant care.

Since Gram had come up from the Cove last month, I'd had a little bit of a reprieve. My grandmother hadn't forgiven her daughter for abandoning me, but out of love for me, she occasionally took a shift sitting with Lorene so that I could get away for an afternoon or an evening. She called it breathing room, and she was right. I needed these few hours when I could escape from the worry and stress of an unpredictable life with my mother.

"Are you sure you're doing the right thing here, Sasha?" From his seat on the top step of the porch, Sam leaned back and frowned at me. "This feels like a risky game you're playing."

"I'm not playing a game." I crossed my arms over my chest. "I didn't exactly lie to Gram. I just failed to correct her when she jumped to a conclusion."

"You're letting her think that there's something between us." Sam skewered me with a sharp gaze.

"Isn't there?" I batted my eyelashes and favored him with a sugary-sweet smile. "And here I thought you loved me."

"Of course, I do." Sam shook his head. "I love you the same way I love Ali and . . . Domino."

"Mr. Nelson's *horse*?" Leaning over, I snatched up my rubber flip-flop and threw it at him. "Nice, Sam. Real nice."

"I'm just saying that we both know there's nothing romantic about our relationship." He stretched out one long, denim-covered leg. "But you didn't stop your grandmother from thinking that there is."

"Nope." I popped the *p* on the word and rocked a little more.

"Even though you know she's probably going to call your boyfriend back in Florida and tell him?"

"The whole point of the plan is Gram calling Cole. I'd be disappointed if she doesn't." I tilted my head. "Sam, I'm not the kind of woman who messes around. I don't want to manipulate Cole. I know I love him, and I trust that he loves me." I hesitated a beat. "At least, he did. He was mad at me when I left the Cove, but I don't think—I hope he didn't stop loving me."

"Sasha, I *do* love you like a sister, and I kind of understand why you made the decision you did—to come to Burton and take care of your mom. But I can also see this from a guy's point of view, and I think that's something you should think about. Cole met you right after your grandmother brought you to Florida, right? He probably remembers what you were like then—I bet you were a scared and defensive little girl. He's known you for a long time, and all those years, your mother has been the person who abandoned you. She's been the villain in your story, or at least one of them."

"Yes." I nodded. "I get that."

"And then you announce out of the blue that you're moving back to Georgia, to a place you haven't been to in over fourteen years, to take care of the woman who left you with an abusive jerk. For Cole, that probably was the craziest thing he could imagine you doing. To add insult to injury, when he expressed his concerns, you told him that his opinion didn't matter—that you were doing it anyway, no matter what he thought. Am I right?"

My eyebrows drew together. "Well . . . kind of. I didn't say that in so many words, but—"

"But here you are," Sam finished. "Actions speak louder and all that. Even if you didn't tell Cole that you didn't care what he thought, you demonstrated it by what you did. That must've hurt. So add up his hurt over what you did, his worry about you and his fear that you might never come back, and . . . yeah, I can understand why he hasn't reached out to you."

"Are you suggesting that I need to be the bigger person and call him? Because if you are . . ." I swallowed. "I don't think I can. I know I act like I'm tough and all that, Sam, but there's part of me that's still the same girl who everyone left. Who no one cared about."

Sam was quiet. I wondered if he was remembering the me from before, the kid he'd known when we were both in elementary school. We'd run into each other a few days after I'd come back to Burton, and I'd been shocked when Sam had recognized me. I'd blocked out just about everyone and everything I'd known from those horrible days, but when Sam had introduced himself, I'd slowly remembered him. Since then, we'd become close friends—again.

I thought our affinity for each other might have something to do with the fact that we were both hurting souls. I was struggling to adjust to a new way of life, caring for a mother I didn't remember, and Sam was still grieving the sudden, untimely death of his own parents four years before. Added to that, he was working almost around the clock to keep the family farm afloat while also raising his younger sister, Ali.

"I can understand how you feel," he said at last now. "Maybe Cole does, too. Maybe he just needs the door opened for him."

"Exactly." I tucked my leg under me as the swing swayed. "That's what I'm doing now. If Gram tells him that he needs to come up here before I do something extreme, like marry you, it gives us a chance to talk. I'll know that he really wants me if he comes to Burton."

"I still don't like it." Sam shifted. "I'm not going to be part of pretending to be your boyfriend or your fiancé or anything like that. If he asks me if I'm in love with you, I'm telling him the truth."

"I wouldn't expect anything else." I rested my chin on the knee of my bent leg. "I don't want to lie to Cole. But I want him to see Burton. I want him to realize that I wasn't crazy to come up here."

"Do you have regrets about coming back to Burton, Sasha?" Sam's gaze was steady. "Taking care of your mom hasn't been a walk in the park."

"No, it hasn't been easy. She's ridiculously demanding even when she's relatively sane, and I can't ever relax. She's unpredictable and emotional and angry. She's never once thanked me for dropping my life to come up and take care of her. When she's in pain, she's nasty and hateful." I took a deep breath. "But I don't regret it. She left me when I was little because she's got a mental illness and because she was addicted to drugs. I can hate that fact, but she's still my mother."

"I can't even imagine." Sam's jaw stiffened. "I remember stuff, you know. I remember when we were kids, and sometimes you came to school with red eyes because you'd been crying all night. I remember that sometimes you wore the same clothes for a week, because no one was around to tell you differently or to wash those clothes. I remember that you walked everywhere, that you never had someone there to pick you up after school." His eyes softened. "My mom asked me one time if I was nice to you. She said you had a hard life. Later on, after you left town with your grandmother, my mother told me that she was relieved. She'd been trying to get you help for a long time, but in a small town, it's not always easy to make people see things they don't want to know."

"It was your mom who finally found Gram and got in touch with her." I'd only learned this fact recently. "I can't imagine where I'd be now if she hadn't done that. I might not even be alive. He was crazy."

"But you're here, and you're healthy and relatively sane." Sam winked at me. "And even if I can't understand any better than Cole does why you came back to take care of Lorene, I'm kind of glad you did, because it means I got to know you again."

I opened my mouth to reply, but before I could, we both heard the rumbling of a car turning down the long dirt driveway that led to the farm house. A Chevy Chevette bumped over the narrow road, coming to a halt a couple of yards from the porch. The passenger door opened, and a pretty girl jumped out, slamming the car door behind her. Her light brown hair danced around her shoulders in soft curls as she paused to wait for the driver of the car, a tall guy in jeans who held out his hand to her before they both meandered toward Sam and me.

"Hey, Ali. Hey, Flynn." The corner of Sam's mouth twitched, and I hid a smile. I knew all too well what my friend was thinking. He was his sister's guardian, the last remaining adult in her life, and he felt that responsibility heavily. He liked her boyfriend, Flynn Evans, as well as any brother might like the boy his baby sister hung all over, but he'd told me more than once that he worried about their relationship.

"They're so damned young, Sasha. And I can't watch them every minute of the day. I'm working in the fields from before sunrise to after sundown. There's too much time when I don't know exactly what Ali's doing."

I sympathized, but privately, I felt as though he was fighting a losing battle. I knew all too well what it felt like to be an eighteen-year-old girl in love with the only man I'd ever dated. I didn't think there was much Sam could do to keep those two away from each other.

"Sam, did you eat all the pie I made today? I wanted Flynn to have a piece." Ali climbed the steps to the porch and nudged her brother's leg with the tip of her sneaker. "Tell me you weren't a total pig."

"There's still pie in there." Sam leveled his eyes at Flynn. "Why don't you bring it out here for Flynn to eat?"

"Nah." Ali flipped her hair over her shoulder and rolled her eyes. "I was thinking I'd take it upstairs to my bedroom and let him eat it off my boobs."

"Nice, Alison." Sam growled the words. "I'm just making a suggestion. Don't be a smartass."

"But you act like we're insatiable animals. Like we're going to take advantage of the fact that we're alone in the kitchen to have hot sex, when you and Sasha are sitting out here on the porch."

"Ali." Flynn's face had gone red, and I felt sorry for him. Being stuck between your girlfriend and her older brother couldn't be easy. "C'mon. Sam's not saying that." He loosened his grip on her hand. "Why don't you bring the pie out here? I'll wait."

"Fine." Ali heaved a long and dramatic sigh. "Whatever." She pulled open the door and disappeared into the house, her footsteps coming close to being stomps.

"I think that's my cue to head back home." I unfolded my legs and stood, stretching my back. "Gram's been on Lorene duty for a while. I don't want to abuse her good will."

Sam groaned. "You're leaving me alone with them? Thanks. I thought you were my friend."

"I am." I patted his head as I passed. "Flynn, be nice to my buddy here. He's trying his best."

The younger man smiled faintly at me. "Yeah, I know. Ali doesn't mean anything. She's just slightly dramatic sometimes."

"Slightly?" Sam snorted. "She could give Meryl Streep a run for her Oscars."

"I think it's kind of cute." Flynn glanced at me, and what I saw in his eyes made suddenly and painfully homesick for Cole. He'd looked at me that same way, once upon a time. He'd thought everything I did was adorable and sexy. I missed that—I missed *him*—more than ever. Considering my heart had been dying by degrees since the day I'd left him in the Cove, that was no small feat.

"Thanks for the listening ear, Sam." I jingled my keys from one finger. "I'll see you this weekend, probably. If I can get away."

"Call me if you need anything." It was the same thing Sam always said when we parted. I never had been forced to ask for his help, but it was nice to know he was there, just in case.

I thought about that as I drove back into town, back to the tiny duplex where I was living with the woman who'd given me life and then left me four years later. Being here in Burton hadn't been easy, but there were benefits I'd never expected. Even though I was a virtual stranger, having been gone for almost a decade and a half, the town had been welcoming and supportive. I'd met people who remembered my mother from years before and who had offered help now. More than once, I'd found bags of food on our doorstep, or someone would pop by to deliver a hot meal.

The years I'd spent living in Crystal Cove had taught me that small communities had both good points and bad. Everyone in the tiny beach town loved my grandmother, who'd moved there years before I was born to pursue her dream of being an author after her husband had died and her daughter had run away. I was known there as Miss Dixie's granddaughter, and that was enough for most people to treat me well. But at the same time, I knew there were others who still saw me as the abused child who'd had to be rescued by Miss Dixie. I felt that shadow following me.

It wasn't different in Burton . . . except, somehow, it was. Everyone I'd met so far had been compassionate and kind. No one mentioned Phil, the man who'd beat me, who'd let me go hungry and who'd made my early childhood a living hell. He'd been in prison for a long time, and although I knew he'd been released, apparently, he'd never returned to Burton. Gram had assured me that he had no connection to the town aside from my mother, and he certainly wouldn't come back now.

Pulling up to the curb in front of the old house, I gave myself the luxury of sitting in the car for an extra few moments, to gather up my strength before I went inside. I hadn't lied to Sam. I didn't regret the choice I'd made to come back here. But still, it wasn't easy, and there were moments when I'd give anything to be anywhere but with Lorene.

There was a glimmer of hope tonight, though. If Gram had called Cole, which, judging from a few telling remarks she'd let slip, I was nearly certain she had, he might be coming up to Burton. He might even be on his way now. And when he got here—I refused to even consider that he might not come—then things would be better. I'd always been stronger with Cole by my side, and I was sure that once he came to Burton and saw the town, got to know the people, he'd fall in love with this community the same way I had.

I just had to make him see that Burton was the perfect place to us to start the rest of our lives together.

Chapter Three

COLE

I'd been to Georgia before, but never to this part of the state. When we were in high school, I'd represented northeast Florida at young leaders' conference in Atlanta. The bus had driven a bunch of us across my home state and then north to Georgia. I remembered thinking that travel was overrated; I couldn't tell where Florida transitioned into Georgia. Atlanta had been a riot, but I'd been just as happy to get home to the Cove.

This time, though, as I drove west from Savannah, I had to admit that there was a certain rugged beauty to the land. It wasn't beaches and ocean and salt air, but there were acres of waving green over dark soil, with neat white houses dotting the scenery here and there.

And when I followed a road that morphed into the main street of Burton, I felt as though I'd taken a turn back in time. Small businesses lined the street, and there was an honest-to-goodness village green complete with gazebos. People were walking on the sidewalks, pausing to talk to each other. It reminded me of Beach Street back in the Cove.

Gram had called me with directions, so I knew how to get to the house where she was staying. As I understood it, Sasha's mother had disability and Social Security payments that allowed them to rent half of a small house that had just enough space for the two of them. When Dixie, worried for her granddaughter's well-being, had come up to check on the situation, she'd accepted the hospitality of an old friend.

That's why I was about to knock on the door of someone named Boomer, who was, apparently, the husband of Gram's friend Millie.

"Cole! Thank God you're here." Gram grabbed my hand and hauled me into the house.

"Hey, Gram." I wrapped the older woman in a tight hug. I'd been raised by loving parents in the lap of a close-knit family, but Dixie Jones had been my surrogate grandmother for as long as I could recall. She'd moved in next door the year before I was born, and from the time I was allowed to leave the house on my own, her home had been a haven, a place where I could go to talk about anything.

And when she'd brought her granddaughter to Florida, that had been the icing on the cake. Sasha had been belligerent and shut off . . . with everyone but me. The friendship we shared had been instantaneous and close from the first time I'd set eyes on her, even if she didn't remember it that way.

That day on the boat, when my dad had taken us both fishing—that wasn't the first time we'd met. Sasha's memories of the early days were understandably fragmented, and she didn't recall that I'd spent time with her at Dixie's house, well before the fishing trip. Even though I'd been grumpy and maybe a little mean that particular day, I'd already known that I liked the odd new girl in town. I'd already felt that connection that never left us.

It wasn't surprising, then, that the last six months had been so painful. It was the longest time we'd gone without seeing each other or without communicating since we were eight years old.

"Come in, come in." Gram took the duffel bag from my hand. "Millie's at work, and so is Boomer, but Christy and Jenna are around here, doing homework. You're sleeping in Carla's room, and I'm in Courtney's." She pointed to the steps. "Right up here."

As we walked down the hallway, two heads poked out of the doors. "Cole, this is Christy—" Gram pointed to the older girl, who I judged to be about fourteen—"and this is Jenna. Girls, this is Cole. He's Sasha's boyfriend."

"Well, I used to be, anyway." I wasn't feeling so confident just now.

"Oh, don't be silly. She loves you. She just needs to be reminded." Gram stepped into the last bedroom on the left and dropped my bag onto the narrow twin bed. "There you go. Do you want to freshen up before we go over?"

"Go over where?" I frowned.

"To see Sasha, of course." Gram rolled her eyes. "That's why you're here, isn't it? And time is of the essence, as they say. You only have a week, and you have a lot of work to do."

"I thought you said she still loves me but just needs her memory jogged." I unzipped the duffel and pulled out a clean shirt. "And how do you know I only have a week?"

"You told me that you took a week off from the Tide, and I assumed it was the same with your job with Daniel. Go ahead and change, and I'll meet you downstairs."

I stared after her as she shut the door behind her. Something was fishy here. Something was off. I didn't have any hard proof, but I had a feeling I was being played.

. . ⚜ . .

"THIS IS WHERE SHE'S living?" I scowled at the tired-looking house that was set behind a tiny lawn of brown grass.

"This was all Lorene's income could support. I told Sasha I'd help them out, so they could live somewhere a little nicer, but you know her. She said she'd rather manage on what they have."

"Typical," I muttered. "Why take help when you can be hard-headed?"

"Now, Cole." Gram laid a hand on my arm. "You can't go in there with that kind of attitude. When I said Sasha needed to be reminded that she loves you, I didn't mean you had to bash her in the head with the idea. You have to be subtle."

I snorted.

"Do you remember when she came to the Cove? When I brought her home, and she sat in that big wicker chair on my porch, curled up and speaking to no one?"

I nodded. I could still see her, red hair cut short as her father had chopped a hunk of it off a week before Dixie had rescued her, her eyes big and sad. I'd come over with my cardboard box of miniature toy cars and dumped them on the deep cushion of the chair.

"Let's play cars."

For a solid ten minutes, she'd simply stared at me, and then finally, she'd picked up a bright blue Mustang that was one of my favorites and begun driving it along the seam of the cushion. Half an hour later, we were both sprawled on the floor, running our cars.

"If you had gone in that day, loud and demanding, Sasha would've withdrawn. But you were quiet and kind. You won her over that way. Not much has changed, Cole. Inside, she's still the same little girl."

"Okay." I blew out a long breath. "I hear you. I'll go in easy. I'll listen to what she has to say."

"Good boy." Gram beamed at me. "All right, come on. We'll head in there. I'll handle Lorene, so you can concentrate on Sasha."

It felt a little like a SWAT operation as we trudged up the walk. I raised my hand to knock on the door, but Gram only shook her head and turned the knob.

"Sasha! It's me." She stepped inside, and I followed close behind.

"I'll be right there." The voice I'd been missing for six months floated from the back of the house. A second later, there was a loud crash of shattering glass and a shriek.

Without stopping to think about it, I launched myself toward the sound, bursting through a closed door at the end of a short hallway. The room on the other side was tiny and dimly lit, but I could still make out the bed against the wall, where a thin old woman cowered, keening as she wrapped her arms around her bony knees.

"Cole?" Sasha knelt in the shadowy corner, surrounded by splinters of glass. "What are you doing here?"

For a long moment, I couldn't answer. I simply stood there, letting my heart beat slow to a more normal pace as I stared down at the woman I'd loved all my life.

Sasha had always been beautiful. Her hair, which had been bright and blindingly red when she was a child, had deepened into a rich shade of auburn. She still wore it short, giving her an almost fey-like air. Her skin was like the finest white sand, pale and translucent. Dixie had been manic about sunscreen and hats when we were kids, because Sasha had such a light complexion that she was at risk for burning during the long hours we spent on the beach.

Yes, my girl had always been gorgeous, but now . . . she took away my breath. Maybe it was that I'd gone so long without looking at her, or maybe her months in Burton had been good for her. Whatever the reason, I couldn't deny that Sasha was simply exquisite.

"Cole." She repeated my name. "Why are you in Burton?"

So many answers flitted through my head, but the loudest was Gram's voice warning me to be gentle. "I came for you, of course. Sasha . . ." I knelt in front of her, carefully avoiding the glass. "I can't go any longer without you."

Tears filled her large green eyes. "You came for me. I hoped . . ." She sniffed. "I thought you would. But I wasn't sure." She shifted gingerly, rising up on her knees. I reached for her, and then—

"STOP!"

The old woman clapped her hands over her ears and screeched the word. "Stop, stop, stop. Go away."

Sasha rose slowly to her feet. "Lorene, it's okay. Calm down. It's not real. You're all right. So am I." She glanced at me. "She hallucinates. For her, the things she sees are as real as you and I are. That's why she threw the glass. She thought she was protecting me.s"

I wasn't sure what I'd pictured when I'd thought of Sasha's mother, but it hadn't been this frail creature. She didn't look anything like her mother or her daughter. Dixie was a feisty, hearty woman, and if I were looking at her and her only daughter side-by-side now, I'd swear their roles were reversed. Lorene looked ten years older than Dixie.

"They're here," she whispered now. "Right behind you. Can't you see them?" She sounded so sure that I was tempted to look around and check over my shoulder.

"Lorene, come on now. Let's take your medicine, okay? You take these pills, and I promise the monsters will go away."

"No, they won't. They're going to eat me. They're going to tear me to shreds, and then they'll come for you."

"I won't let that happen." I stood up, too, my feet planted wide. "You let Sasha help you, and I'll stand guard."

Sasha began to speak, but I held up a finger. Lorene was listening to me. Her face was troubled and unsure, but I could tell that she was considering what I'd said.

"I've dealt with these kinds of monsters before," I assured her. "I know how to take care of them. You do what Sasha says, and I won't let anything happen to either of you."

Lorene's eyes flitted to her daughter, and Sasha took advantage of the wavering to inch closer. "Open your mouth and take a drink of this water. Let me take care of you."

Obediently, Lorene allowed Sasha to give her the medication. I never moved, standing guard until she had settled back down with her head on the pillow.

"You won't let them get me while I sleep?" Her voice was sluggish.

"No. I promise," I answered.

Sasha and I stood still until Lorene's eyes were shut and her breathing was regular. Sasha nudged me and pointed toward the doorway. Once we were in the hall, she closed the door quietly behind us.

"Thank you for that." Her cheeks had flushed, either from the effort of dealing with her mother or from embarrassment that I'd witnessed the scene.

"It wasn't a problem." My fingers itched to bury themselves in her hair, to tug her close to me, to kiss those full lips . . . but I held back. "Do you have time to talk?"

Humor sparkled in her eyes for a moment. "You drove all the way up from the Cove. If I didn't make the time to talk to you, I'd be a pretty poor excuse for a friend."

I swallowed. "Is that all we are now?"

Sasha jammed her fingers into the front pockets of her faded denim shorts. "Haven't we always been friends? I thought we were. I thought we always would be."

"Of course. But I hoped we were more."

In the living room, a few steps away, Gram cleared her throat. "If you want to go somewhere to catch up, I'll sit with Lorene."

Sasha looked torn. "I'd love to, but she'll probably only sleep an hour or so, and then she'll need her dinner and her second set of meds before she goes down for the night."

"And you don't think I'm capable of doing that?" Gram shook her head. "Please. There may have been a lot of years between then and now, but she's still my daughter, and I know how to handle her. You two get out of here and talk to each other. I didn't do all this work to maneuver you together for it all to go to waste."

We both turned to stare at Dixie. "*You* did all the work?" Sasha sputtered. "That's bullshit. I'm the one who made you think—" She stopped speaking abruptly, pressing her lips together.

"That you were sweet on Sam Reynolds? Good golly, Sasha. I've known you for a long time, and I've always been able to read you like a book. You were no more in love with that dear man that you are with Boomer. And I know when someone is trying to play me. I was well aware that you wanted me to raise the alarm with Cole, to get him up here. But I didn't mind doing my part, because it's high time the two of you stopped being stupid."

"You called and told me Sasha was going to marry that farmer." I shook my head. "Gram, you lied to me."

She smiled serenely. "I didn't lie so much as I presented a set of circumstances in a particular light. If you hadn't come to Burton, Cole, Sasha may very well have ended up marrying Sam, just because he's a wonderful man and a good friend to her. I'm only trying to keep everyone from being hurt." She pointed at me and then at Sasha. "*You* belong with *her*. Go work it out."

Sasha's eyes flickered my way. "We could walk over to the green. It's a nice afternoon, and we could talk."

I nodded. "Lead the way."

As we made our way down the path toward the sidewalk, Gram opened the screen door and called after us.

"Don't come back here until you're holding hands and kissing like fools!"

Chapter Four

SASHA

"This is a beautiful town." Cole gazed around the green as we sat down on the bench in the gazebo. "I can see why you like it."

"I didn't expect to feel at home here. Not as much as I do." I pulled up my knees and wrapped my arms around them. "I know I talked it up before I left the Cove, but the truth is that I thought I'd come back, and if I had any memories of this place at all, they'd be bad ones. I figured everything that had happened to me there had been horrible. I expected nightmares and people pointing me out as the kid who'd been taken away from her father."

"But . . ." Cole prompted.

"But a few days after I got here and settled Lorene into the house, I went to the hardware store and ran into Sam." I smiled. "He looked at me and said, 'Hey, Sasha. Is that you? Been a long time.' I couldn't believe he remembered me. And then I started to remember him, too. Some happier memories came back—of times when people were kind to me. And just about everyone was so welcoming. They've reminded me that this is a good town."

"The Cove is a good town, too." Cole's knee jiggled, and I didn't miss the way his jaw clenched. "It's the town that took you in when you didn't have anyone else. It's *my* town. It's where I live. It's where our future is."

"I love the Cove, too." I wasn't sure I could explain how I felt, but I had to give it a try. "But I'm not sure I want to live there."

Cole was silent. I could almost feel the hurt emanating off him in waves, and my heart contracted.

"This has nothing to do with you. It isn't about us." Reaching out, I slid my hand into his, entwining our fingers. "I love you, Cole. I always have, and I always will. When I think about the future, I see us together. It's what I want."

"But all the plans we've discussed have been set in Florida." He tightened his hold on my hand, even though I heard the caution in his tone. "You just finished college. I've been working for Jude since I was sixteen and for Daniel since we graduated high school. I'll finish with my degree in December. We've saved up just about enough to open our own restaurant, like we always said."

"I still want all of that." I twisted to face him, clasping his hand between both of mine. "But why can't we have it up here, in Burton?"

"Because we live in Crystal Cove. That's our home. Why would we move up here?" Cole was stubborn when he was certain that he was right.

I sighed and stared out over the expanse of grass. "Lorene is going to need me for a while, Cole. A couple of weeks ago, at her regular appointment, the doctor told me that I need to consider moving her into a facility, where she can have round-the-clock care. I don't want to do it, but what you saw a little while ago—that was a mild example of how she is. It's getting worse. She's violent sometimes, and more than once, I've been scared."

"That's even more reason for you to come back to Florida. Get your mother settled into the nursing home, and then you can come back to where you belong."

"I can't just abandon her here, Cole." I rested my head against the back of the bench. "I know what you're thinking. You wonder why I feel so strongly about it when she didn't have any qualms about leaving me. But I'm not like her. That's one thing I've learned in the past six months. Lorene might be my mother biologically, but we don't have anything at all in common."

"You wouldn't be abandoning her. We can come up and visit as often as you want." Cole lifted our joined fingers to his lips and kissed the back of my hand. "I promise."

"I know you do. But Lorene is just one piece of the puzzle. The truth is that I love Burton, Cole. I can see us here. If you spent a few days and gave it a little time, I think you'd understand."

"I'm not saying this isn't a great place. But it isn't home." Cole laid his hand alongside my cheek, framing my face. "Crystal Cove is home."

"It's *your* home. Burton is where I was born. It wasn't all a horror show. And since I've been back, it's felt right to be here. Please . . . just think about it."

"Sasha, are you trying to say that this a deal breaker? We haven't seen each other for six months, and here we are, sitting next to each other, discussing where we want to live like we're a couple of strangers or business partners. I haven't even kissed you yet." He nudged my chin up so that I was gazing into his eyes. "And Sasha, babe, I'm dying to kiss you. To hold you."

A flood of warmth and want filled me, threatening to overflow. "What the hell are you waiting for, then? Kiss me."

Cole's fingers raked into my hair, tilting my head back before he lowered his lips over mine. The moment he touched me, everything in my world that had been wrong and off-kilter for six months fell into place again. The hurt deep inside me eased.

His tongue teased the seam of my lips, and I opened to him without hesitation. The hand that wasn't buried in my hair slid down my back, pressing me ever closer against him. I wanted to climb over him and feel every inch of his skin next to mine. I was hit with the realization of how much I'd missed him and how much I'd craved his lips, his hands . . . and all the rest of his body.

"This." He murmured against me. "This is home. God, Sasha, I love you. I've never stopped, and I'm never going to stop. The other stuff—we'll figure it out. Just promise that you'll never leave me again."

"Never. But you promise, too. Promise you won't make me choose, Cole. Because I love you so much that I can't imagine living without you. And if you make me decide, I'll always choose you. Only I won't be whole and happy. I won't be the person you love." I brushed my hand over his cheek. "Let me be the woman you love."

He eased back a bit and stared down at me, his expression unreadable. When he finally spoke, his voice was gentle.

"I don't want you to be anyone other than who you are. I'm not sure that Burton is right for us. I still feel like the Cove is our place." He touched the tip of my nose. "But we'll talk about it. And I promise to keep an open mind."

I wrapped my arms around him and held on tight. "That's everything I want. Give me a week to show you all the reasons why our future should start right here."

"All right." Cole nodded. "One week."

Anticipation made me laugh in sheer joy. This was a challenge I couldn't wait to accept.

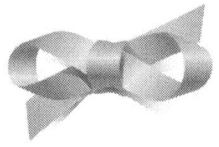

Chapter Five

COLE

For the next five days, I felt as though I was living inside an unending sales pitch for the town of Burton, Georgia.

I realized early on that more people than I'd thought were in on this scheme to make me fall in love with the town. It seemed that everywhere I turned, someone was waiting to explain why everything was better in Burton.

At the local diner, where Gram took me for breakfast, Darlene, the woman behind the counter, greeted me loudly.

"You must be Sasha's guy. Well, we just love her. And she tells Kenny and me—" She hooked a thumb toward the kitchen. "Kenny's my husband, and we own this joint together. Anyway, Sasha told us that you want to open up a restaurant, too."

I felt a little put on the spot. Surely this woman wouldn't be in favor of me starting up a business that would be her competition. "Well, ah, I mean, it's a thought we've had. I'm not sure, though, if we'd do that here."

She scowled at me. "Why the hell not? Burton needs more restaurants. Right now, it's just us and the pizza place. When I want a meal that I haven't cooked myself, I have to haul my cookies all the way to Farleyville, and who has time for that? Nah, you should do it. There's more business in town than you might imagine. And Kenny and I aren't afraid of a little competition." She winked at me and chortled. "Bring it on, brother. We'd be happy to give you some tips about being in the business, too. I have a couple of properties in mind, when you're ready to take a look."

By the time I'd enjoyed my chicken fried steak, I had a real estate listing of several available buildings in my hand as well as the number of the local zoning board and who I needed to talk to about licensing on the state level.

It was the same story everywhere. Gram sat with Lorene for a couple of hours each day so that Sasha could show me around the area, and I was astonished at how many people seemed to know my girl.

At the library, the librarian, Cory Evans, greeted us both with hugs. She told me about her daughters who were in college, one studying business administration and the other veterinary medicine. Her son was about to graduate from high school.

"Burton is the best place to raise kids," Cory informed me. "The schools are small, the neighbors all watch out for each other . . . I wouldn't live anywhere else!"

At the bakery, Kiki Payton, the exotically beautiful owner, offered me a rich chocolate cupcake and some advice. "Don't close your mind to the possibilities in life. Eight years ago, I brought my niece here to raise her after my sister died. It was the best decision I ever made."

Even Boomer, the reticent mechanic in whose home I was temporarily staying, offered me his input. "You move here, you'll never have to worry about your car breaking down. I take care of the vehicles around here, and I'm the best."

It was all a little overwhelming, and I was beginning to wonder about the dark side of a town where the residents were hellbent on persuading someone new to move in. I was tempted to ask Gram if she and Sasha had been indoctrinated into some kind of cult.

On the fifth morning of my visit, Sasha picked me up at Boomer and Millie's house bright and early. Her smile was wide and full of mischief.

"Today I'm taking you to meet my very first boyfriend."

I slapped my hand over my heart as we drove. "Here I thought I was your first."

She laughed. "You were. I'm only teasing. But Sam was my first best friend. I want you to know him."

"Hmm." I frowned. "Are you sure he's not in love with you? And he doesn't think you're going to marry him?"

"No on both counts. Sam loves me the same way he does his baby sister. And he has no interest in marrying anyone, let alone me. He's wholly absorbed in running his farm." Sasha side-eyed me. "I never told Gram I was going to marry him. I might have hinted that he was more interested than he is."

I squeezed her hand. "Once I thought about it, I wasn't seriously worried that you were going to tie the knot with a guy you'd only known for half a year. But it gave me the kick in the pants I needed to get up here. I didn't like hearing about you getting cozy with anyone else but me."

"You have nothing to worry about." She shot me a sunny smile, and the last knot of tension inside me eased a bit.

Sam Reynolds was every bit the decent man he'd been described to be. I could feel the love he had for the land as he showed me around the farm. He pointed out the work he'd done over the past four years, since he'd been forced to take it over after his parents' death. I had to admit, there was a certain appeal to the strong roots he had there, and although my own ran just as deep in Crystal Cove, I was beginning to see the beauty of this part of the world.

When Sasha went inside with Sam's sister Ali, Sam and I stood together alongside a fence as he showed me a new grove of peach trees.

"She's putting the screws to you, isn't she?" He smirked at me. "Sasha, I mean. She wants to stay here, and she's trying to talk you into it."

I blew out a long breath. "Yeah. She has her reasons, and I understand on one level why she wants to live in Burton. But everything we've been working toward is in the Cove. I've always assumed we'd open our restaurant there. We have friends to help out, and people know us. It seems crazy to think about starting over in a brand-new place."

"With a mother who's out of her mind and who never did anything to earn the loyalty Sasha is showing her now," Sam added. "I get it. Maybe I get it even more than you do, because I remember what it was like when Sasha was living here before. I hated losing my best friend when I was eight, but even then, I was relieved that she'd gotten away from that monster. And any woman who left her baby with a dude like him . . ." Sam shook his head. "But like it or not, Sasha's finding some kind of healing here that she might not ever have found otherwise. By taking care of Lorene, she's demonstrating that she's not the same woman her mother was. I think it's been good for her. And although I understand your worries, I have to say I hope you two end up settling in Burton. It just feels right."

I thought about what Sam had said later, while I lounged on the glider in the backyard at Boomer and Millie's home. Sasha was back with Lorene at her own house, and Gram was inside, helping Millie with dinner. Although I could hear the bustle in the kitchen, the serenity of the large yard was pleasant and restful. If I closed my eyes, I could almost picture living in a house like this, with Sasha cooking next to me, running the restaurant alongside me, raising children together and making a life here.

My cell phone rang, interrupting my ruminations, and when I saw the name on the screen, I smiled.

"Hey, Daniel. Is this a get-your-ass-back-to-work call?"

There was a warm chuckle on the other end. "Hey, Cole. Nah, it's not that. We miss you, don't get me wrong, but I was just checking on you and seeing how things are going up there in Georgia. How's Sasha? Did you manage to win her back?"

I stretched my legs out in front of me as the glider swayed. "Everything with Sasha is wonderful. I didn't need to win her back—turned out that I'd never lost her to begin with."

"Not surprised by that. Jude told me from the start that Dixie was exaggerating the situation to get you up there and make you two kids talk. I'm glad to hear it."

"Yeah." I paused. "Daniel, Sasha wants to stay up here. There are a lot of reasons why—and most of them are good ones—but the long and the short of it is that she's asked me to consider moving to Burton."

"Ah." Daniel still didn't sound shocked, but that was typical; my boss was one of the most laid-back men I'd ever known. There was a certain settled air about him, a certainty about his place with his woman, his business and his community. I envied him that. "And what are you planning on doing, Cole?"

"Not sure. I told her I'd take this week to think about it and keep my mind open. She's been putting on the hard sell—actually, it feels like the whole town has. And you know what? You'd love it here, Daniel. The place is enough like the Cove to feel like home. It just doesn't have the ocean and the sand."

"But it does have Sasha." I could almost hear the smile in Daniel's voice. "Cole, that one thing trumps anything else. I get it."

"I'm still not sure that leaving our family and friends and coming to a place where I don't really know anyone is the right answer." I kicked at a clump of grass. "What if it's a huge mistake?"

"Then it's a mistake you'll make together," Daniel answered promptly. "And you'll figure out the answer together, too." He was quiet for a moment. "You know, Jude and I were together just about as long as you and Sasha when we got married. We'd known each other since we were kids. We'd been sweet on each other from the start. When we decided to get married after high school, when we were only twenty, there were plenty of people who thought we were both crazy. I was starting up a business, and we knew that eventually, Jude would have the Tide to run. I'm not going to lie—it hasn't always been easy. When we lived in that tiny apartment above the RipTide—the one where you live now—we got on each other's nerves plenty. Then Meggie came along, and things were even more crowded. Most of my friends were still single, and here I was on Saturday nights, with an exhausted wife and a crying baby."

"Did you have doubts? Regrets?" I knew that Daniel and Jude had been together forever, but I'd never considered that their early years might have been tough.

"Of course, I did. I wouldn't have been human if I hadn't. But at the end of the day, as long as Jude and I were together, I figured I was winning. Even if we'd snapped at each other, even if we went to bed fuming—we still went to bed together. It didn't matter what else was happening in the world—we had each other. It wouldn't have mattered if that was in the Cove or Miami or New York City—I would've gone anywhere Jude wanted, if it meant being with her. That's love, Cole. It doesn't mean abandoning your dreams, but sometimes it means making adjustments to accommodate the other person's dreams, too. It means compromise."

The last piece of uncertainty I'd been holding onto began to disintegrate. "Do you think we can make a go of it up here? Am I good enough to start up a business here, even without the support of everyone back home?"

"You'll have our support, no matter what," Daniel answered. "We might not be stopping in to see you on a daily basis, but I promise—all of us down here will have your back. You can move up there to Georgia, Cole, but you'll always be a Cove boy. And we don't forget our own."

When I hung up the phone, I was filled with a new buzz of energy. For the first time in six months, I knew what I needed to do—and exactly how I wanted it to happen.

Now it was time to put my plan into action.

Chapter Six

SASHA

"What's going on, Gram?" I crossed my arms over my chest and shifted in the car seat to glare at my grandmother. "And where's Cole? I thought he was coming with us."

My grandmother only shrugged. "I don't know, do I? I'm not the boy's keeper. I only know that Sam invited us out to have dinner on the farm tonight. He said he and Ali wanted to celebrate the first harvest of spring. When I asked Cole, he said he'd meet us out here."

"Are you sure Millie's going to be okay with Lorene?" I'd given my mother her medication and settled her for the evening before we'd left, but still . . . I worried. Lorene was becoming more and more unpredictable. I'd been out to visit a couple of the local care facilities, and she was on a waiting list for my favorite one. It wasn't the situation I wanted, but I understood that she needed more dedicated attention than I could provide.

"Of course, she is." Gram rolled her eyes. "Sasha, would you just relax for one night? People want to help. Let them."

I was quiet for a few moments. "Gram, if—and I know this is a big unknown at this point—but if Cole and I end up living here, will you move back, too?"

My grandmother glanced at me. "I've given that some consideration, Sasha. I think the answer is no. Not now, at least. I still love the Cove. I know that Burton is my own hometown, and Crystal Cove is only the place that adopted me after your grandfather died and your mother ran off, but it's still mine. I'll come visit you here as often as I can, but I'm keeping my house in Florida." She winked. "Besides, you'll need a place to come down and stay when you want a beach fix."

I sniffed a little. "I'll miss you."

"Sure, you will, and I'll miss you, too. But we won't be far from each other. You'll have your wonderful life, and I have my own, you know."

"Thank you, Gram." I reached across to squeeze her hand. "Thank you . . . for loving me. For rescuing me all those years ago. For giving me a loving home and the most magical childhood any girl could want."

"I have a lot of regrets, you know, Sasha." Gram sounded a little emotional, too. "If I hadn't left Burton after Lorene ran away, I would've known when she came back with you. I could've prevented those years when you were at the mercy of that man."

"It wasn't your fault, Gram," I argued. "Lorene and my father told everyone around here that you knew about me—that you knew where we were and that you refused to have anything to do with us. I'm just glad that Sam's mom eventually tracked you down anyway."

"I'll never stop being grateful for that—and for the fact that I had all the wonderful years with you that I did. This isn't an ending, Sasha. It's just a brand-new beginning. You remember that."

As she spoke, she turned down the dirt drive that led back to Sam and Ali's house. There were a lot of cars in the yard—more than I would've expected. And something else was weird.

Lanterns were everywhere—hanging from the porch and the trees and lining the edge of the grass.

Gram stopped the car and pulled the keys from the ignition. "Come on. We don't want to be late."

"Late for what?" I felt a little as though I'd fallen through the rabbit hole into a new and unfamiliar wonder land. For all the cars here, I didn't see anyone standing outside, and the house was dark. What was going on?

"For that new beginning I was talking about." Gram tugged my hand, leading me around the house, following the trail set by the twinkling lantern light. As we came around the corner, I stopped suddenly.

All of the people I'd been wondering about—the people who belonged to the cars in front—were gathered here, in the farmyard. They were all looking at me now, and there was a smile on just about every face. Sam broke away to walk toward me, holding out a hand.

"Right this way, Sasha. Don't drag your feet."

The crowd parted, and in the middle of the cleared area stood Cole. He wore khakis and a dress shirt, and although I could tell he was fairly buzzing with nerves, his eyes never left me.

In those eyes, I saw certainty. I saw trust. I saw love.

I saw our future.

Somehow, I was standing next to him, and he took both of my hands in his. "Sasha, the day you came to the Cove was the day our friendship began. I've loved you since the moment I saw you, and I've never stopped. I'm never going to stop." His voice was hoarse, and he cleared his throat before going on.

"I thought it mattered where we lived out our dreams, but now I know that the where isn't the point. All of my tomorrows are right . . . here." He laid a hand over my heart. "You are the only one I want to share those tomorrows. I love you, Sasha. You are my home, and that's the only truth that matters."

Tears blurred my eyes. I couldn't speak over the lump in my throat.

"Sasha . . ." Cole dropped down to one knee and dug into his pocket, pulling out a small box. "Will you marry me? Will you start our future here, tonight . . . with all of the people who will be part of our lives around us now? Will you help me build our dreams together?"

I sank down to the grass and wrapped my arms around Cole. "Yes. Yes, yes, a trillion yeses. I love you, Cole. I love you so much."

Around us, everyone broke into cheers and applause. But for me, nothing else existed except for the man I loved, kissing me as though his life depended on it.

"I love you, Sasha. Forever and then some."

The End

Or . . .

Just the beginning.

The Burton Gazette

The biggest news in town this week is the opening of a brand-new restaurant right here in Burton.

Smoky Joe's Barbecue debuted on Friday night, with lines out the door and around the corner. Initial reviews are glowing.

Owners Cole and Sasha Wilson reported that opening weekend diners exceeded their wildest expectations.

"We are both gratified and overwhelmed by the response," local girl Sasha remarked. "And we are so thankful for the help of our friends and neighbors, particularly Darlene and Kenny, who gave us invaluable tips about running a restaurant in this town."

Sasha's husband Cole hails from a small beach town in Florida, where he worked for years at a family-owned eatery. He met his wife while she lived with her grandmother, former Burtonian Dixie Jones. The two relocated to Burton last year, after their wedding in Crystal Cove, Florida.

"We've needed a new place to eat around here," said local mechanic Boomer Sutton. "I'm glad we have more than one place to choose from now."

Smoky Joe's is open six days a week, from noon until nine, with extended hours on Fridays and Saturdays. Take-out is available.

Notes about Burton and Crystal Cove

Some years ago, I wrote my first contemporary romance, which took place in a small Florida beach town. Crystal Cove continues to be the setting for that series of romances.

However, in the first book, the main character Jude had a daughter whose summer residency program took her to a rural Georgia town . . . Burton. That book (*The Last One*) kicked off the *Love in a Small Town* series.

The *Crystal Cove Romances* and the *Love in a Small Town* series have continued to overlap and cross-over, so when I decided to write this prequel, it was only right that it should include both communities.

If you want to know what happened to Sam Reynolds, as well as to his sister Ali and her boyfriend Flynn Evans, you're in luck. If you want to know more about Jude and Daniel and Logan and Meggie . . . good news! I've got you covered.

The following is the recommended reading order for the books.

Love Me Home (A Love in a Small Town Prequel)
The Posse (A Crystal Cove Romance)
The Last One (Love in a Small Town #1)
The First One (Love in a Small Town #2)
The Only One (Love in a Small Town #3)
The Plan (A Crystal Cove Romance)
The Perfect One (Love in a Small Town #4)
The Path (A Crystal Cove Romance)
Always For You (Love in a Small Town #5)
Underneath My Christmas Tree (Love in a Small Town #6)
Always My Own (Love in a Small Town #7)
My One and Always (Love in a Small Town #8)

Always Our Love (Love in a Small Town #9)
The Love Song Girl (Love in a Small Town #10)

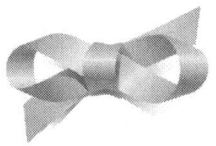

A Peek at
The Last One

"DON'T LET HER INTIMIDATE you. She's been doing this since she could walk, pretty much." Sam's voice behind me made me jump.

I straightened and looked at him over my shoulder. He was working on the row to my left, and he didn't pause as he spoke.

"She's fast." I shook the dirt off the next onion and laid it in the basket. "I'm afraid I'm not much help."

He flickered his eyes to my face briefly. "You came out to help. That counts. We're doing well, actually. Should finish up tomorrow."

"Does that mean you'll be around the house more?" I blurted out the words and felt my face heat. "I mean, you won't have to work so hard, right?"

Sam laughed, and I smiled in spite of myself. I hadn't heard that sound before, and it turned out that he actually had a pretty great laugh.

"Summer on a farm means all hard work. No let up, really. But yeah, I'll be around a little more. I won't have to run off after dinner every night." He slanted me another glance. "Why, did you miss me?"

"Don't flatter yourself." I smirked. "I don't even really know you. "But I was afraid maybe you were avoiding me. I don't want to make things difficult for you."

Sam straightened and stretched his back. "Like you said, we don't really know each other. We got off on the wrong foot, and I jumped to some conclusions. I'd have to be pretty stupid to let you push me out of my own house just because of that."

I smacked my forehead where a particularly aggressive mosquito was attacking. "Okay. Just checking. Because if I do make you uncomfortable, I can always see about living somewhere else this summer. There's got to be another family who'd host me."

"Don't you like living out here? What's the matter, not exciting enough for you, city girl?"

I dropped another onion in my basket. "See, that right there, that's what's wrong with you. You come over here, you're nice to me, sort of, in your own special way, and then you say something like that. You don't know anything about me, as I think we established that day at Boomer's, but you make assumptions. For your information, I love it out here. I couldn't think of a better place to spend the summer. The farm is beautiful, and I want to explore it. I want to paint the orchard at sunset and that empty side pasture at sunrise. Ali's been sweet to me, and I love Bridget already. And I'm not a city girl. I go to school in Savannah, and yeah, it's bigger than Burton, but it's hardly New York City, is it? I grew up on the beach. Oh, and I might be slow at onion harvesting, but I'm a damned hard worker."

"Whoa, there." We'd come to the end of the rows, and Sam held out one hand toward me. "Nobody said you don't work hard. You're the one who brought up moving."

"Only because I'm trying to be nice, dumbass!" I stamped my foot, which in the soft dirt had far less effect than I might have wanted. "I'm giving you an out. To say—yes, Meghan, you make me uncomfortable and I don't like you, so take your stupid self off to another place."

He frowned and glanced over the field. "I didn't say you were stupid."

I set my jaw and rolled my eyes. "Oh my God, you are the most irritating man. Fine. I'm not stupid, and I work hard." It struck me what he hadn't denied. "But I do make you uncomfortable? Why? Because of the drinking still? I promise you, I don't make a habit of it. You don't have to hide the vodka while I'm here."

"No, not because of the drinking. I told you, I realized I was wrong to say what I did that day. Your friend—Laura—she told me you didn't get drunk very often."

"Then what is it?" My basket was getting heavy, and I set it on the ground, rolling my shoulders. Sam's eyes dropped to my chest as the motion drew the cotton T-shirt tight over my boobs. I watched in fascination as his Adam's apple bobbed, and he licked his lips. *Interesting.*

"I don't know." He closed his eyes and ran a grimy hand through his hair, leaving it standing on end.

"If you don't know why I make you uncomfortable, then I don't know how to stop doing it." I took one deliberate step closer to him, standing on the lumpy ground where the onion plants had been. His eyes widened slightly, and he stiffened.

"Are you more uncomfortable now, Sam?" I realized this was the first time I'd called him by name. It gave me an odd thrill. "Does it make you nervous when I stand this close to you?"

He looked down into my eyes as though he had no other choice. "Only because you smell like bug spray and onion juice."

I let a smile curve my mouth, and I stood on my tip-toes so that my lips were even with his ear.

"Liar."

I stepped back, still smiling, as Ali came over. "What's going on?"

"Nothing." I picked up my basket again. "Sam was just giving me some pointers."

"Really?" Ali didn't look convinced, but she only held out a hand to me. "Here, let me have your basket. I'm taking mine over to the truck. Just get a new one and you can start on the next row, if you want."

"No problem." And because he was still standing there motionless, I made it a point to step close enough to Sam that my arm brushed him as I passed.

Just because I could.

Other Books by Tawdra Kandle

Fearless
Breathless
Restless
Endless
The King Series Boxset
Undeniable
Stardust on the Sea
Unquenchable
Death Fricassee
Unforgettable
Death A La Mode
Death Over Easy
Moonlight on the Meadow
The Fox's Wager
Age of Aquarius
The Posse
The Plan
The Path
The Last One
The First One
The Only One
Love in a Small Town Box Set Volume I
Love in a Small Town Box Set Volume II
Always For You
Underneath My Christmas Tree
Always My Own
My One and Always

Always Our Love
The Love Song Girl
Best Served Cold
Just Desserts
I Choose You
Just Roll With It
When We Were Us
Hanging By A Moment
Days of You and Me
Not Broken Anymore
Maximum Force: A Career Soldier Military Romance
Temporary Duty: A Career Soldier Military Romance
Hitting the Silk: A Career Soldier Military Romance
Zone of Action: A Career Soldier Military Romance
Damage Assessment: A Career Soldier Military Romance
Scheme of Maneuver: A Career Soldier Military Romance
Fifty Frogs
The Anti-Cinderella

ABOUT THE AUTHOR

Tawdra Kandle writes romance, in just about all its forms. She loves unlikely pairings, strong women, sexy guys, hot love scenes and just enough conflict to make it interesting. Her books include young adult and new adult paranormal romance, new adult and adult contemporary romance and adult paramystery romance. She lives in central Florida with a husband, kids, sweet pup and too many cats. And yeah, she rocks purple hair.

Did you love *Love Me Home*? Then you should read *Fifty Frogs* by Tawdra Kandle!

Boy meets girl. It's the way romances usually begin . . . and while we all love a happy ending, it's the #MeetCute that wins our hearts.

How did you two meet?

The #MeetCute Books each have a unique answer to that query. Some might make you swoon, others might make you giggle . . . and some may make you blush.

Twelve authors. Twelve stand-alone contemporary romance novels. Twelve stories that will make your heart beat a little faster.

Because it's all about the #MeetCute.

Vivian is sick of dating. Sick of the way guys treat her, sick of living and crying by when and if they call . . . she's just done.

When her aunt reminds her that a girl has to kiss a lot of frogs before she finds her prince--Aunt Gail says that number is fifty--Vivian decides she's taking control of her dating life: she's going to go on a series of first dates only, and each one must end in a kiss. She begins chronicling each date--the good, the bad and the downright unbelievable--with a plan to turn the stories into an in-depth magazine series about the realities of dating in the twenty-first century.

Everything's going along according to plan until Vivian hits a bump in her road with Frog Number Five, who doesn't seem to understand his role in this deal. And despite Vivian's determination to make it all the way to the big five-oh, when fate keeps throwing this same man across her path, she begins to wonder if maybe it's time to ditch the plan . . . and kiss just one more frog.

Read more at tawdrakandle.com.

Made in the USA
Lexington, KY
20 May 2018